June's New Shoes

by Marcy Kelman
illustrated by Aram Song

Disney
PRESS

New York

La La La

It was a lovely spring morning. While Annie, Leo, and Quincy waited for their friend June to arrive, they each did their favorite things: Annie sang, Leo conducted, and Quincy played the violin.

When June arrived, Annie noticed something different about her. "Wow, June!" exclaimed Annie. "Are you wearing new ballet shoes?"

"Yes, I just got them this morning," June said, beaming. "Aren't they beautiful? My old shoes were so comfortable, but I wore holes right through them with all my dancing. Wearing new shoes feels a bit strange, but I'm sure I'll get used to them." *What kind of shoes are you wearing right now? Are they old or new? Do you have a favorite pair you like to wear?*

"These new shoes make me feel like dancing. Don't you just love to dance? Let's all do a twirl together. One, two . . . OUCH!

"Oh, dear. I was afraid that was going to happen. Every time I try to leap or twirl, I fall!"

Poor June. Can you help cheer her up? GREAT!

Hummingbirds always make June happy.

Let's take a walk down Hummingbird Lane. First we have to find the sign with the hummingbird on it. Is it the first sign, the second sign, or the third sign? Yes, it's the second sign! Thanks for helping us find Hummingbird Lane.

It worked! The dancing hummingbirds helped to put a big smile back on June's face. It looks like she is going to try a hummingbird flutter over the stone wall. Now it's your turn to flutter: can you flap your arms really fast like a hummingbird?

Oh, dear. June fell down again. Luckily, the team was there to catch her.

"Don't worry, June," said Annie. "We're here for you. Just take your time, and you'll be dancing before you know it."

"It takes time to get used to new things," Quincy said. "When the bow for my violin broke, I never thought I'd get used to playing with a new one. I hit one or two wrong notes at first, but the more I played, the better I got! Just listen." **Zim-zim-zim-zim**!

Leo agreed. "I remember the first time I wore my glasses. I knew I needed them to help me see things clearly, but they felt really strange at first. It took a few days to get used to them, but now I don't know what I'd do without them!"

Did you ever have a hard time getting used to something new?
Everyone has!

Look! Rocket is sending a signal to the team. Someone needs their help. Let's check the screen on the Look-and-Listen Scope. What do you see? It's the moon! Who is standing on the moon? It's the Little Einsteins' friend, Cow. She was trying to jump over the moon but didn't quite make it.

"Team, we have a mission," said Leo. "Cow is stuck on the moon, and it's up to us to help get her down!"

"But how did she get up there?" asked Annie.

"Aha! Rocket is showing us Mount Everest—the tallest mountain in the world," replied Leo. "Cow must have leaped from the very tip of the mountain, but instead of jumping over the moon, she landed right on it."

"Poor Cow," said June. "I know how it feels when your leaps don't work out the way you planned."

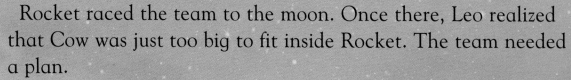

Rocket raced the team to the moon. Once there, Leo realized that Cow was just too big to fit inside Rocket. The team needed a plan.

"I've got it!" exclaimed Leo. "June, you're the only one who can help Cow jump back down onto Mount Everest."

"It's true, June," agreed Quincy. "You're the best dancer we know. You can do it!"

"Oh, dear," replied June. "I'm just not feeling so sure of myself today. Do you really think I can do it?"

June wants to leap over the moon, but she needs our help. *Will you help us? GREAT! Let's sing to June and cheer her on!*

We know you can do it, June.
We believe in you.
You can do a ballerina leap
To help Cow get off the moon!

They made it! June and Cow landed safely on Mount Everest. "Hooray," said June. "We did it! I just needed time to get used to my new shoes and to get my confidence back. Thank you all for believing in me!"

Oh, dear. Cow is still very far from home. She doesn't belong on Mount Everest. We need to get Cow back to her home. *Do you know where cows live? Hmm, let's check the screen on the Look-and-Listen Scope for a clue. Do cows live in the desert, in the jungle, or on the farm? Yes, you're right! Cows live on farms. Oh look, that must be Cow's farm at the bottom of the mountain.*

"Cow is back home!" cheered Leo. "Mission completion!"
"I think it's time for a hoedown, partners!" shouted Quincy.
"Let's celebrate with a song," said Annie.
"And a dance!" added June.

Hey, diddle, diddle,
Quincy's on the fiddle.
June jumped over the moon.
We knew she'd know how
To help our friend Cow.
We believed in you, June!